W9-AAZ-505

GOT BRAINS?

by Emma T. Graves

illustrated by Binny Boo

STONE ARCH BOOKS
a capstone imprint

Published by Stone Arch Books
A Capstone Imprint
1710 Roe Crest Drive
North Mankato, Minnesota 56003
www.mycapstone.com

Library of Congress Cataloging-in-Publication Data is
available on the Library of Congress website.

ISBN: 978-1-4965-6447-4 (library binding)
ISBN: 978-1-4965-6451-1 (paperback)
ISBN: 978-1-4965-6455-9 (ebook)

Summary: Undercover zombie Tulah is excited
to join the academic bowl team . . . until she
remembers her nemesis, Bella Gulosi, is captain!
When the group goes on a retreat, keeping her
undead secret becomes even tougher, and Bella
is crankier and meaner than ever. How can
Tulah survive the weekend?

Editor: Abby Huff
Designer: Brann Garvey

Printed in the United States
PA017

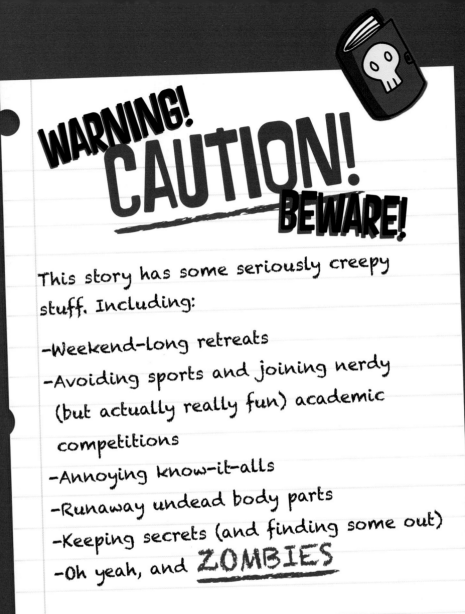

WARNING! CAUTION! BEWARE!

This story has some seriously creepy stuff. Including:

-Weekend-long retreats
-Avoiding sports and joining nerdy (but actually really fun) academic competitions
-Annoying know-it-alls
-Runaway undead body parts
-Keeping secrets (and finding some out)
-Oh yeah, and ZOMBIES

Keep reading if you want, but don't say I didn't warn you.

7

CHAPTER 1

Underneath the dining table I could hear a soft *thump, thump, thump.* My dog, King Kong, was wagging his tail. My French bulldog's life had gotten a lot better since mine ended. It turned out zombies made great pet owners!

For one, I'd started a dog-walking business (to pay for the meat I had to eat to keep from acting like a monster). That meant King was getting outside and sniffing all the smells.

Two, I couldn't sleep anymore. So I was up every night to serve all King's emergency belly-rub needs.

And three, since I couldn't stomach cooked food, King got a lot more scraps under the table. Good thing he wasn't a picky eater.

I slid King a bite of broccoli and looked around the dinner table to make sure nobody had noticed. My parents were busy haggling over the week's carpool duties. My little brother, Jaybee, was gobbling everything on his plate and playing his own sneaky game.

Jaybee was reading a comic book he'd hidden on his lap. He was always reading a comic or watching a show. No matter which one it was, it was sure to be about monsters.

The little geek was the only one in my family (besides King) who knew I wasn't among the living. TBH, his knowledge of all things zombie had been a major help in figuring out my undead life. I don't think I could've kept my "life status" a secret without him. And keeping my life status a secret? That was crucial!

I had learned early on that dead people made living people super uncomfortable. And if you were *walking* dead? People would FREAK OUT. If anyone, including my sweet parents, discovered my heart wasn't pumping? They would do whatever they could to put me six-feet under, and I was not ready for that.

I mean, I just started middle school!

I wasn't saying my parents didn't love me. But they felt very strongly that their twelve-year-old daughter should:

1. Keep her room clean

2. Engage in only two hours of screen time per day

3. Get good grades

4. Participate in extracurricular activities

5. Be ALIVE

OK, they never said that last rule out loud. But I *knew* how they felt about the rest, and I felt like the last one was a safe guess.

"So, Tulah are you ready for cross-country to start?" Dad asked when he'd finished sorting out the driving schedule with Mom. He looked at me with his eyebrows raised and his eyes sparkling.

I moved my jaw up and down, pretending my mouth was full. I gave Dad a tight-lipped smile. He grinned, thinking that meant "yes." But inside I was screaming "NO!"

I knew this was coming. There was no escaping rule number four: participate in extracurricular activities. My last school activity, the musical, had wrapped up a while ago. And Dad had been chomping at the bit for me to join the Evansville Middle School cross-country team. You see, he was the coach. Now I was finally there.

"I've got some great ideas for the team this year," Dad said. "I want to get us off on the right *foot*!"

"*Uuugggghhh*," I groaned, and not just because of the silly pun.

When I was alive, I loved running. I was good at it. But zombie Tulah was stiff and awkward, which wasn't great for any kind of sport. Worst of all, I didn't heal. If I got injured, I had to be stitched back together like a worn-out teddy bear!

Lucky for me, my friend Angela's family owned a funeral home. Angela was an expert with dead people. She had already helped a ton with keeping my corpse stitched up and fresh.

But cross-country? That was too big a risk for this zombie. One fall and I could lose a limb. Five falls and I could end up looking like a patchwork quilt!

I needed to find a way to quit the team before I'd officially joined.

Mom squinted at me from across the table. I was pushing around my cooked chicken (yuck!) and trying not to make eye contact with my parents. She could sense my lack of excitement.

"It'll be good to get you back into an activity," Mom said in a tone that meant, "You *need* to get back into an activity."

All I could do was nod. Avoiding cross-country might've been easy if: My dad wasn't the coach. My mom wasn't a lawyer who was only convinced by super solid arguments. And they weren't both strong believers in rule number four.

"Oops!" I said as I accidentally-on-purpose swatted the last bite off my plate.

It flew into King's waiting mouth. He slurped up the food while I excused myself to do homework. I needed an argument to get out of cross-country, and I needed it fast.

When I was alone in my bedroom, I started a group chat. I needed to talk things out with Nikki (my BFF since forever) and Angela (my BFF since death).

ME: *Having a crisis. Dad is still expecting me to be on the cross-country team.*

NIKKI: *Crisis? What's the problem with cross-country?*

ANGELA: *The problem is that if T falls, she'll get totally torn up. And T will TOTALLY fall.*

NIKKI: *Oh, riiiiight! Maybe you could just wear ski pants and a parka while you run. That'd protect you. :)*

ME: *:/ Seriously. How can I get my parents to let me quit without it seeming like I'm quitting?*

NIKKI: *What about academics?*

ME: *Huh?*

ANGELA: *Huh?*

NIKKI: *The Academic Team! It meets after school on Tuesdays and Thursdays, the same days as cross-country. We're one kid short from having two complete teams, and Ms. del Toro would LOVE to have you. Plus you'd be with meeeeeee!*

ME: *The A Team! OMG, that might work. I wouldn't be quitting. I'd just be joining something else. Nikki, you're a genius!*

An academic activity might be the only thing in the Jones house that had a chance at beating cross-country. (See rule three.) It was brilliant. Plus the trivia quizzes and competitions of A Team seemed like fun.

ME: *Thank you! You two put the B in BFF.*

NIKKI: *IKR?*

ANGELA: *ROFL (but not literally). TTYL.*

I set down my phone and took out a pen and a notebook. All I had to do was craft my argument—the way my lawyer mom taught me. If it all went well, I'd be able to keep my body safe inside a classroom answering questions instead of risking injury on a rocky trail.

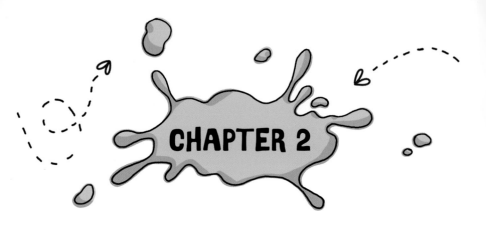

CHAPTER 2

"OK, *now* can you tell me?" Nikki asked as soon as Angela stepped onto the bus the next morning.

"Almost," I said with a smile. "We have to wait till Angela is actually sitting down."

I had been holding off telling Nikki my parents' ruling on the case of *A Team vs. Cross-Country.* It had been too late to call last night. Besides, I wanted to see both of my friends' faces when I gave them the news.

Angela slid into the seat ahead of us, and I immediately blurted it out. "My parents agreed!" I said. "I can join the A Team and quit cross-country!"

Nikki squealed and bounced up and down. A smile spread across Angela's usually serious face. They were both happy for different reasons. Nikki was happy because I'd be on the A Team with her. Angela was glad I wouldn't end up on her embalming table in need of repairs—so long as I was careful about paper cuts and staplers.

"You guys should've seen me," I said. "I was calm, cool, and collected."

Of course, being dead helped. My zombie nerves of steel were the best side effect of being reanimated. I didn't get anxious like I used to. My new nerves allowed me to perform onstage, not act like a dork in front of my crush, and make my case to my parents without shaking. (None of that would've happened if I were alive.)

"I marched in while they were watching TV and laid it all out," I continued. "At first, my dad looked disappointed. But then I pointed out that joining A Team would probably lead to debate team in high school. And how debate team would look really great on college applications. They both got excited and agreed!"

"That's awesome news," Angela said.

"You're telling me," Nikki said. She was still bouncing. "With you on A Team, I'll finally have someone to complain to about Bella Gulosi! I mean, she's super smart. But she's definitely not the most encouraging or supportive team captain."

The moment Nikki mentioned that name, I felt my smile melt.

"Oh *noooooooooo!*" I moaned, slapping my hand to my forehead. "I completely forgot about Bella!"

Bella Gulosi was the most competitive person I had ever met. She always had to be the smartest and the best at everything.

Unluckily for me, after I beat her in the fourth-grade spelling bee, she had decided that I was her greatest competition. Since then she had done everything possible to make sure she won . . . and I lost.

One time she told the teacher I was cheating on my math test. (I wasn't.)

Teacher!

She stole my science fair project idea.

Oops!

And she once "accidentally" spilled milk on my history homework so it'd be marked late (and she'd get the highest grade).

To say Bella and I weren't friends was an understatement. She was my enemy number one.

Nikki saw the look on my face. "Come on, Tulah," she said. "We can deal with know-it-all Bella. It's better than running cross-country and losing a knee."

"Yeah. Bella can't be that bad . . . can she?" Angela asked.

I looked at the back of Bella's head, five rows ahead of us on the bus. I looked at my knee.

Maybe doing A Team with my nemesis will be better than losing a knee, I thought. *Maybe not.* But what choice did I have after convincing my parents to let me join? Absolutely none.

"Tulah Jones, is that you?" Ms. del Toro asked as Nikki and I walked into her classroom on Tuesday after school. She clapped her hands. "Does this mean what I think it means?"

Just as Nikki had predicted, Ms. del Toro was excited to see me at A Team practice. At least *she* was happy, because Bella Gulosi sure wasn't.

"I hope not," Bella muttered, shooting me one of her nasty looks. "Don't you have *jogging* practice or something, Tulah?"

I ignored her jab, and Ms. del Toro didn't hear it. The A Team coach was busy looking at the approval form I had given her.

"Everything is in order!" she said. "Welcome to the team! We were just hoping for one more person to join. Bella, isn't this wonderful?"

"Absolutely thrilling," Bella replied. Somehow Ms. del Toro missed the sarcasm. I didn't.

When Ms. del Toro's back was turned, Bella walked over to Nikki and me. She poked me in the chest. "Don't get any ideas, Tulah Jones," she hissed. "I joined A Team first. This is *my* activity. You can't just waltz in and take over."

I glared back at her. "Who said I was taking over? Besides, I thought this was a team activity. I just want to be a part of it."

"Whatever," Bella said, scowling. "Just don't forget, I'm the captain because I'm the *best*."

Nikki saluted Bella. "Ay, ay, Captain!" she said jokingly. Then she grabbed my arm and pulled me away. "Don't worry. Bella will warm up to you when you help us win."

I looked back at my nemesis. The idea of her warming up to anything seemed unlikely. There was nothing warm about her. Bella's skin was so pale it was almost blue. TBH, she looked a little sick. I felt grateful that, as a zombie, I couldn't catch whatever cold Bella must've had.

It looked like everyone else was keeping their distance too. Bella sat by herself near the window while the other students gathered by the bookshelves.

Bella noticed me watching her. "I suggest you stop staring and start studying, *Tulah*.

In A Team we work hard. It's not like some stupid school play, you know."

Nikki rolled her eyes. "Just ignore her," she said. "Come on. You have to meet everyone else."

We slid into seats next to the other A Team members. They were much more welcoming. Lacey, Chris, Josh, Vincent, and Braden all cheered when they realized I was joining. They were super helpful too.

"Here," Lacey said. She slid her notes across the table to me. "We usually start with a warm-up study time. Then we play some speed rounds, which are like quizzes."

"You won't have to do the speed round today, though," Nikki told me. "Ms. del Toro never makes new members go up on their first day."

I nodded, relieved. I wasn't nervous, but I liked to be prepared.

Ms. del Toro walked to the front of the room. "All right, A Team. I want you all to welcome Tulah Jones to our squad!"

Six kids clapped. Bella got busy looking for something in her backpack.

"I have something very important to discuss with Principal Moody," Ms. del Toro said. "So I'd like you to practice on your own today. Bella, you're in charge."

Ms. del Toro's last words were the last words I wanted to hear.

The door had barely clicked shut when Bella strutted to the podium and clapped her hands. She loved giving orders. "Listen up, A Team. This is how it's going to go. You've got five minutes to study and come up with three questions. Then it's the speed round. Tulah, you'll go first."

"But—" I started to protest.

Bella cut me off. "You heard Ms. del Toro." She tapped on her phone to set the timer. "I'm in charge."

CHAPTER 3

I quickly read over Lacey's notes. As I flipped through them, I thanked my unlucky stars I didn't get nervous the way I used to.

"Time's up!" Bella shouted as soon as her phone timer sounded. "Let's go, Tulah. We're all waiting!"

Bella tapped her fingers on her table impatiently. I knew she was trying make me nervous. The old (living) me would've been shaking like Jell-O. And Bella knew it.

So my nemesis looked surprised as I walked calmly up to the podium. No sweaty palms or pounding heart would throw off my game today. This zombie was as cool as a cucumber!

"You will answer five questions. You have fifteen seconds to answer each one," Bella told me from her seat at the side of the room. I swear she was smiling as she started the timer. She was still expecting me to choke!

"Go!" Bella pointed at Vincent. "Read the first question!"

"This, uh, scientist supposedly caused an earthquake with his oscillating m-machine," Vincent stammered. "He made a namesake coil that creates electricity. He—"

Easy peasy. "Nikola Tesla," I said.

I grinned.

Bella frowned.

"Braden, let's have a math question." Bella pointed at a boy from my algebra class. She restarted the timer.

Braden read his index card. "George and Martha are each planting a garden. George's garden is four feet long and three feet wide. Martha's is a square with two-foot-long sides. What is the total area of the two gardens?"

"Sixteen square feet," I said.

Nikki gave me a thumbs-up, and I did a tiny victory dance. Without my nerves, A Team was just as fun as I thought it'd be!

Two correct answers later it was Bella's turn to ask the question.

She flipped through her cards, no doubt looking for the hardest one. A smile slowly spread across her face as she took out a card.

"In this book, Elizabeth Lavenza is murdered by the creation of her adopted brother, Victor," Bella read. "Victor's creation sees his reflection and realizes he's hideous, sending him into a murderous rage. What is the book by Mary Shelley whose title character is the doctor, not the monster?"

"*Frankenstein!*" I said right away.

Bella must've thought I didn't know horror stuff. But as an undead girl, I had already studied up on all the classics.

The team clapped. Bella glared at me. I smiled back. I wasn't going to let her get under my skin, even though it seemed like she was doing all she could to sabotage me.

"Nikki, you're up next," Bella barked.

I cheered on Nikki as she nailed all of her questions. The other kids took their turns too. Soon only one person was left.

"You're up, Captain!" Lacey gestured toward the podium as she stepped away.

"I *know*," Bella snapped. She rolled her eyes and stumbled on her way to the front of the room.

For someone who was getting exactly what she wanted (she was IN CHARGE, after all), she sure seemed cranky.

Braden read the first question. "This type of gamete is produced in the stamen and is transported to the pistil," he said slowly. "It's made in the flowers and cones of plants. Name the powdery substance used for plant reproduction that causes many allergies."

Bella didn't answer. She just scowled. "Can you repeat the question?" she asked.

Braden read it again, even slower. I could see the answer on the lips of every kid on the team.

But Bella didn't say anything.

She just stood there looking angrier . . .

. . . and angrier.

Time!

I can't believe Bella didn't get "pollen."

For once Ms. Know-It-All . . . didn't!

"Change of plans!" Bella yelled as she stomped back to her seat. "Silent study time for the rest of practice."

"But Bella didn't even finish her round," Nikki muttered.

"Because she knew she was going to flub it," I whispered back.

"What don't you understand about *silent* study?" Bella said, shooting us a glare.

The room quieted as everyone took out their notes. I shared with Nikki.

A silent half-hour later, practice was almost over. Kids were starting to gather their stuff when Ms. del Toro burst back into the classroom. She had a grin on her face.

"I have great news!" she said. "Principal Moody told me we got funding to go to the academic team retreat at Young University!"

Everyone around me started cheering.

"Wait. What's that?" I asked Nikki.

"It's like A Team vacation!" Nikki said. She grabbed both of my hands. "We're talking three days together at YU, with lots of other academic teams. It'll be so rad. We'll get out of school on Friday. Then we do team building, practice, play games. We sleep in the dorms, and eat together, and . . . oh . . ."

Nikki trailed off. She had realized everything she thought was great wouldn't be so fun for a member of the walking dead.

"Sleeping and eating together?" I said. "Three days with *Bella*?"

"It'll be super fun?" Nikki said, sounding a bazillion times less excited than she had five seconds before.

The team started heading for the door. Ms. del Toro handed each of us a permission slip as we filed out. "I need these back right away. I know this isn't much notice, but we'll leave this Friday morning for the retreat. What a dream come true, right?"

I shoved the slip in my bag and tried not to look freaked out.

The A Team dream sounded like a zombie nightmare.

CHAPTER 4

"A two-night sleepover? There's just no way!" I moaned.

Angela took two of the five dog leashes I was holding. With her free hand, she awkwardly patted my shoulder.

I had been panicking all day Wednesday during school. But I hadn't managed to come up with a way to avoid the retreat. I knew I needed help.

So I'd asked my favorite gloomy goth to help me walk the dogs and talk over my issue. The pups were now happily pulling us down the sidewalk. (Angela easily walked, while I lurched and lumbered.)

"OK. First things first," Angela said.

"What exactly scares you about going on the retreat?"

"For one thing, I don't sleep!" I answered. Of course she already knew that. "If people see me just lying in my bed, wide awake for eight hours . . . well, it could get pretty suspicious."

Angela nodded slowly. "We can figure something out for that," she said calmly as she untangled Mop's legs from Count's leash.

Angela was like that. If there was a problem, she wanted to find a solution. Ever since she figured out I was a zombie, I had been her main problem to solve.

We turned into the park and slowed down. The pack of dogs had lots of smells to explore here.

"Plus, there are just so many things that I need to do while I'm not sleeping," I whined. "All the stuff I do at night helps get me through the day. I've got a whole routine!"

37

"How am I going to get my stuff done when I'm sharing a room?" I asked.

"I'm not sure," Angela said. "You're definitely going to have to pretend to be asleep, though. At least for a while."

"I won't even be able to get *out* of a bed if I stay in it too long. I'll be so stiff that I'll be a log!" The more I talked, the more I started to panic. "Plus, just lying in a dark room doing nothing all night? I might die of boredom!"

"That's not even possible," Angela said. "You're already dead, remember?"

"Oh, well that makes me feel better," I mumbled.

The dogs pulled us through the park, and we walked without talking for a few minutes.

"So, when do you leave?" Angela finally asked. I could almost see the gears turning in her head, and it almost made me feel better.

"Friday, at the start of school. We come home Sunday," I told her.

Angela nodded and untangled Mop from Count's leash . . . *again.* I wondered if she felt like she was always untangling my troubles too. I wondered if she ever got sick of it.

"Let's get these dogs home," she said. "I need time to come up with a plan."

I crossed my fingers, being careful with the pinky Angela had already stitched back on once. I hoped she could save me again!

The next day at A Team practice, everyone was excited. Except me. And Bella. Our captain looked paler and angrier than ever and was still sitting by herself.

"At the academic retreat we'll get to play against teams outside of our regular meets," Ms. del Toro told us. "So, today I want to break into two teams and review the format of the match."

"This is gonna be so good!" Nikki said as she rubbed her hands together. She tucked away facts like a squirrel collects nuts. She loved showing off her random knowledge. "I can't wait for the retreat!"

I slumped farther into my seat. I could wait forever!

At lunch Angela had told me that she was still working on a plan, but she wasn't ready to let me in on it yet. It hadn't sounded very encouraging.

"Nikki, Tulah, Braden, and Vincent. You're one team. Bella, Lacey, Chris, and Josh, you're the other," Ms. del Toro said, interrupting my thoughts.

We got into our groups. Ms. del Toro stood at the front of the table.

"We don't have buzzers, so raise your hand when you have the answer," she said. "As you know, the clues get easier as the moderator reads more of the question. The earlier you answer, the more points you can receive. If you're wrong, the moderator will continue reading, and the other team has the chance to respond. Sound good? Then let's get started!"

Our teams were ready to face off. Bella glared at me from across the table.

41

It was weird. From the look on Bella's face, I would've thought she was trying her hardest. Her forehead was wrinkled. The tip of her tongue was sticking out of the corner of her mouth. It looked like she was thinking so hard her head would burst.

But it wasn't doing her any good.

It wasn't like Bella not to know a single answer. Usually she knew *everything*. I wasn't the only one who noticed, either.

"What's up with Bella today?" Nikki whispered during a break. "She used to be the brains of this outfit."

I shrugged. "I don't know. Unless . . . you don't think she's so mad at me for joining the team that she's sabotaging all of us?"

Nikki's eyes got really big. "No way. Bella hates to lose," she said.

But when I went back to the table, I caught Bella glaring at me as if she wished she could shoot lasers from her eyes. Right then I wasn't sure what Bella hated more—losing or me.

CHAPTER 5

"Rise and shine!" Mom said. She poked her head into my room at 6:30 a.m. the next morning. "Today's the big retreat!"

"*Mmmmm,*" I groaned and rolled over.

I'd been up all night (as usual), but this time I hadn't gone through my regular routine. Angela still hadn't told me how I could survive the weekend, and I'd decided I couldn't risk it. Not with so many people around, and definitely not with an angry Bella staring at me 24-7. I needed a way out.

So after doing my yoga, I'd skipped the makeup. Instead I had grabbed a towel and had run it under hot water. For the last half-hour, I had been using the wet cloth to warm my forehead.

"I don't feel good," I moaned.

"You don't look good!" Mom said as she came closer. She put a hand on my clammy forehead, like I knew she would. "You're burning up!"

I laid it on thicker. "But I *can't* be sick. I'll miss the retreat."

"Sorry, sweetie. If you have a fever, you'll have to stay home," Mom replied.

"I can't let my team down," I pretended to argue. But inside my head I started doing victory laps as Mom stepped back into the hall. I thought she was on her way to call Ms. del Toro to let her know I wasn't going to make it. But a minute later Mom was back . . . with a thermometer!

I sat up fast.

There was no way I could let Mom take my temperature. No matter how much I warmed up my forehead, my insides were as cold as the grave. Well, they were probably more like room temperature, but still. My real temperature was NOT NORMAL!

As soon as the thermometer beeped, I grabbed it and lumbered back to Mom.

"Huh. It's perfectly normal," Mom said when she saw the readout. She reached to touch my forehead again. I dodged.

"Guess I better get ready!" I dashed to the bathroom before she could say anything.

Hanging out with living girls for three days was risky, but it was better than my mom finding out I was dead!

After I slapped on some corpse makeup, I lurched back to my room. I quickly threw my makeup and some clothes into a duffle bag. I was packing so fast I almost forgot underwear! I hoped I wasn't forgetting any zombie essentials. Now I was *really* hoping Angela had come up with something good.

"I'm off!" I shouted toward the kitchen. My parents came rushing at me with hugs.

"Wow, you already look so much better!" Mom said.

"So proud of you, honey," Dad said. "Go get 'em!"

I hoped he'd still be proud when this was all over. "Debate team" might look great on a college application, but "Death certificate"? Not so much.

I hurried out the door. Nikki was waiting at our bus stop. She was loaded down with her weekend gear.

"Don't look so freaked out!" Nikki said when she saw me. "It's not like this retreat is going to kill you."

"Very funny," I mumbled.

"You'll see," she said, still grinning. "We're going to have fun."

We piled onto the bus with our stuff. When Angela got on, she was dressed all in black (like always). But she was carrying a bright red backpack I had never seen before.

She took the seat in front of Nikki and me. Then she plopped the bag into my lap.

"I made you a Bug Out Bag," Angela said, smiling. "It'll get you through the weekend."

Nikki and I looked at her blankly. "What's a—" Nikki started to ask.

"A Bug Out Bag, or BOB, is a pack with everything a person needs to survive for seventy-two hours," Angela explained. "People make them in case of emergencies, like earthquakes and fires. Only Tulah's BOB is for surviving sleepovers."

I unzipped the bag and peered inside. It was filled to the brim with gear for the walking dead!

Tulah's Bug Out Bag (BOB) supplies:

Map of YU campus

Thermos of embalming smoothie

Superglue

Headphones

Eye mask

Super-strong breath mints

Sewing kit

Meat jerky (hidden in energy bar wrappers)

"The headphones and eye mask are to get you through the night. Tell the others you can't sleep without them. I sent some links to podcasts to your phone. They'll keep you from getting bored," Angela explained.

I nodded.

"The thermos has extra-strength embalming smoothie in it. Drink just a little each day. It has to last until Sunday," Angela said.

I nodded again.

"I also packed freeze-dried meat," Angela added. "If anyone asks why you aren't eating the university food, tell them you have allergies."

I kept nodding as Angela took out a map of the campus. She pointed to a red X. "The gym is open all night," she said. "If you can get there, it'd be a great place to stretch. Go between two and five in the morning. That's when most people are sleeping deeply. Even if you stumble around the room, they probably won't notice anything."

Inside the bag there was also a sewing kit and superglue for emergency repairs. I even had mints to help cover up the pickled smell of the embalming smoothie.

I never should've doubted Angela. She had thought of everything! By the time we pulled up to school, I had nodded so much I thought I might be turning into a bobblehead doll.

We filed off the bus with all our bags. I could see Ms. del Toro waving beside a school van. The rest of the A Team was gathered around nearby. Most were standing in a circle and talking excitedly. Bella stood off by herself, looking grumpy.

I took a deep breath and slung the red BOB over my shoulder. I felt like Batman getting equipped by his butler, Alfred. Only I wasn't fighting criminals. All I had to do was keep my deadness under wraps.

I turned to Angela. "Thanks for always bailing me out," I said. "I couldn't do this without you."

Angela shrugged, as if saving my undead life was no biggie. "I told you I'd figure something out. Besides, I like helping my friends."

I hugged her stiffly, and she hugged me back just as stiffly. "Loosen up," I joked. "People will think you're a zombie or something."

Angela smiled. "Right. Call or text me if you need anything." She waved to me and Nikki as she headed into the school.

Next to the van, Ms. del Toro was getting her clipboard ready. "All aboard!" she called.

Nikki put an arm around my shoulder. "Ready?" she asked.

"As I'll ever be," I replied.

With Nikki by my side and Angela watching my back, I felt like maybe I really could get through this.

CHAPTER 6

"When are we going to get there?" Braden asked for what was (I'm pretty sure) the nine-hundred-thousandth time.

"Soon, I hope!" Lacey said. She leaned close to the open window. "Seriously, did the football team leave their sweaty jerseys to rot in here, or what?"

A two-hour ride in a cramped school van was never going to be fun. But it was made worse by the van's funky stench. Nikki had even spritzed some of her perfume, but Candy Dream wasn't enough to cover the stink.

Ms. del Toro waved toward the window. "Ta-da! How about now?" At long last we were turning into the entrance of Young University. Ms. del Toro pulled to a stop.

"We're a bit late, so we've missed check in. Just leave your bags on the van for now."

Nikki plopped her bag down. I did the same with my duffle, but slung my BOB onto my back. No way I could leave that behind.

"She said to leave the bags, Tulah," Bella said in a snotty voice. She was turned around in her seat, looking at me with an eyebrow raised.

"Thanks, I heard." I adjusted my BOB. "But I can't leave my laptop. My life would be over if anyone got their hands on this bag," I explained. I didn't have my computer in there, but the rest was true.

Bella rolled her eyes and stood up. She pushed through the other A Team members. She was so eager to get off that she stumbled and almost face-planted in the parking lot. Lucky for her, Josh caught her by the arm just before she smacked into the concrete.

But was she grateful? Nope! Bella quickly yanked away from Josh without so much as a thanks.

Two kids back in line, I kept a firm grip on the seats. I didn't want to need a rescue of my own. I was pretty stiff after the long ride.

Once I was safely outside the van, I shuffled over to Nikki and the others. Ms. del Toro talked to a retreat leader while we stretched and looked around.

The YU campus was big and green. Tall buildings surrounded a central quad. Paths led off to more buildings in the distance.

"This way!" Ms. del Toro called to the team. We followed her into a classroom.

About thirty other students were already inside. They were huddled in three groups around large tables. An instructor waved us to an empty one.

"Hi!" the instructor said in a whisper. "We're glad you made it. Settle in and let's get started." She handed us a packet. "Each team has to correctly answer as many questions as possible in twenty-five minutes. How you do that is up to you and your team captain. Good luck!"

Bella grabbed the questions and started looking through them.

"Here, let me help." I reached for the packet of cards, but Bella pulled back.

"I can do most of these myself," she said.

"There's no way you can do all of them. Why don't we split them up and work in pairs?" I said. "Two heads are better than one, and we can answer more that way."

"It depends on whose heads we're talking about," Bella huffed.

"I like Tulah's idea," Josh whispered. "Divide and conquer!"

Reluctantly Bella handed half the cards to Josh. He quickly divided them up among the rest of the team. Lacey, Nikki, and I worked together. The boys worked in twos.

I sorted my group's cards into topics. "Let's all take what we're best at," I said.

"Perfect!" Lacey said. "I'll take math."

"History for me, please!" Nikki said.

I took the science questions and got to work.

We were done in no time. Soon the boys were high-fiving too. Bella was still scowling at her pack of questions, and there were only four minutes left.

"Bella, we can take some of yours," Nikki whispered.

"Or check your answers?" Lacey asked.

Bella didn't even look up. "I got it," she said. But she just kept flipping through the cards.

"That's time!" the instructor called. "Let's go over the answers. Please check your own work."

Of the fifty questions, Josh and Braden got six. Lacey, Nikki, and I got nine. Chris and Vincent got seven. Bella held twenty cards, but she wouldn't show us how she did.

"OK, team captains. Please raise your hand if your team scored twenty or more," the instructor said.

All four hands went up, including Bella's.

"More than thirty?" the instructor continued.

Bella's hand went down. The rest stayed raised up.

Everyone on the A Team looked like they'd been punched in the gut. We had come in dead last. The top score was more than double ours.

"Well, that's not a great start to the weekend," Braden muttered.

I looked over at Bella. I thought our fearless leader might be kicking herself for trying to do too much on her own, but she just looked kind of . . . confused. She was silent for the rest of the session.

At noon we went outside for lunch. The retreat people gave us brown paper bags with sandwiches, chips, fruit, and cookies. Nothing I could swallow.

I took the bag and settled on the lawn by the rest of my team. But I set the lunch aside and pulled my thermos out of the red backpack from Angela. I took a few gulps of the embalming smoothie and unwrapped a piece of beef.

Bella watched me from across the circle. "What, you're too good for the sack lunch?" she asked, finally finding her voice.

"Allergies," I said. "You just never know what's going to have a nut in it."

Bella squinted at my dried beef. She leaned closer and wrinkled her nose. "I didn't know you had allergies. And I thought you were a vegetarian," she said. "That looks like meat."

Bella knew I used to be a vegetarian because she was one too. We used to both get the meatless options. She stared as I tore off another piece of beef. It was creepy.

I swallowed the bite of meat. "I was, but my doctor was starting to worry about my protein levels."

On the other side of me, Nikki nodded. My BFF acted like it was a story she'd heard a thousand times before.

But Bella was still silently studying me. It almost felt like she was waiting for me to get out more of my freeze-dried treats. She looked . . . hungry.

"Do you want my lunch?" I held out the brown paper bag of stuff I couldn't stomach.

Bella instantly pulled away like I'd just offered her mud. "No way!" she yelled.

"Aren't you going to eat, Bella?" Nikki asked. "It might help you think more clearly."

"I'm not hungry," Bella snapped. "And I'm thinking just fine!"

Nikki and I exchanged a look.

Lacey leaned closer to Bella. "Are you sure you're feeling OK?" she asked.

It was what everyone on A Team was wondering. Our captain had been looking so pale and acting so strangely. Everyone stared at her.

"If you want, I can go get Ms. del Toro," Lacey added.

"I AM FINE!" Bella said too loudly. "Leave me alone. All of you. I'm just not hungry! I don't need any help from anyone."

With that, our team captain stood up and stomped away in a huff.

CHAPTER 7

"Our first dorm!" Nikki grabbed my hand. "I always knew we'd be roommates in college. But I thought dorms would smell better. . . ."

"Me too," I said. Nikki was right. The room definitely had a weird funk. "It's like the smell from the van is following us."

"I'm on it," Lacey said. She went over to the window and started prying it open. Bella stood silently in the corner with her arms crossed.

I sighed. *Too bad Nikki isn't my ONLY roommate,* I thought.

The four A Team girls were staying in one room. The four guys were in the neighboring dorm building. Our room was pretty much what I expected. Two sets of bunks and four desks.

I tossed all my bags on a bottom bunk as quickly as I could. I needed to be low so I could easily sneak out.

"I'll take top!" Nikki said and put her pack on the bunk over mine.

Lacey claimed the other top. That meant Bella was on the bottom . . . right across from me.

I frowned, thinking of the way Bella had snapped at lunch and how grumpy she'd been through the afternoon sessions. I didn't really like working with her either, but she didn't seem to understand we were on the same team.

When we got our stuff settled, the four of us went down to the cafeteria for dinner. Ms. del Toro had encouraged us to get to know the other teams, so Nikki and I sat with kids from Amityville Middle School. I was more than happy to get away from Bella.

After dinner the retreat leaders told us the evening activities. They'd be showing a movie in the common room and having a Trivia Party game night in the cafeteria.

"Let's do the movie. I can't answer another thing!" Nikki said dramatically, putting a hand on her forehead.

"I'm just up for anything that keeps me out of bed," I whispered. Even with the helpful gear in my BOB, I wasn't looking forward to the first night.

When the movie ended, we took our time getting back. Lacey passed us in the hall. She was on her way to the bathroom with a toothbrush and towel.

"Be quiet when you go into the room," she told us. "Bella's already in bed, and she's in a rotten mood!"

"Isn't she always?" I asked.

"No, this is bad even for her!" Lacey whispered. She paused. "I really hope she's not sick . . . or that she gets better soon. We need her for the Sunday tournament!"

"Yeah," Nikki agreed. "But if she's not feeling good, she should go home. She's no help like she is."

"True. I swear you'd be a better captain than she is, Tulah, and you just joined a week ago!" Lacey said.

Nikki snorted. "OMG. Wouldn't it just *kill* Bella to hear that?"

I laughed too—sort of. It was more like a chuckle and cough combined. Because something about the whole Bella situation felt off. I just couldn't put my finger on it.

When Nikki and I went into the room, we tried to be quiet as we dug through our bags for pajamas and toothbrushes. But we weren't quiet enough for Bella. She sighed, rolled over, and covered her head with a pillow.

Good, I thought. *Keep your head covered. That'll just help me sneak out tonight!*

Unfortunately when we came back from the bathrooms, Bella was uncovered again. She was glowering at the bunk over hers.

"Goodnight!" I whispered.

"Nighty-night!" Nikki said.

"Night," Lacey said.

"Whatever," Bella grumbled.

I felt a little jittery as I put the headphones over my ears, slid the mask over my eyes, and pressed PLAY on my phone. *Here goes nothing!* I thought.

An hour later, I knew one thing—Angela was a genius! The podcast link to *Terrifying Tales from History* she'd sent was a perfect distraction (and included some good history facts to boot). I was lying in the dark, not freaking out, not bored, just . . . still.

Three hours later, after I had learned all about the Medieval Ages, I could feel my muscles stiffening. I knew I had to get up soon. I pressed PAUSE and listened for my roommates' breathing.

Nikki was quietly snoring in her cute way. Lacey was whistling a little out of her nose. Bella wasn't making a single noise.

I peeked out from under my sleeping mask. Bella's eyes were closed. Now was the time to make my move.

I lifted back the covers and *s-l-o-w-l-y* swung my feet over the edge of the bed.

The mattress squeaked. I paused. I waited to see if anyone would stir. No one did, so I stood up.

The floor creaked under my feet. Every tiny noise sounded like it was being blasted through a concert sound system!

I grabbed my duffle bag and gently set it on the bed. I pulled the blankets over the bag and hoped the lump looked like me. Or enough like me that nobody would realize I was gone if they glanced over.

Ms. del Toro had warned us earlier.
If anyone was caught out of their room
for anything other than a bathroom break,
they would be sent home. Immediately.

I slipped one hand through the strap on
my BOB. Then I turned the door handle and
pulled it open as gently as I could with stiff
muscles.

Once I was on the other side of the door,
I closed it just as slowly.

The latch clicked. I waited for what felt
like an eternity, listening for any sounds in
the room. It was quiet as a grave.

I was free!

I pulled the map out of my BOB before
slipping it onto my back. Then I started my
lurch down the hall.

I moved as quietly as I could, but I couldn't help stumbling a little. I hadn't been that still for that long in a while.

But the farther I got from Bella and our shared room, the better I felt. I was really doing this!

The gym wasn't far from the girls' dorm, and I didn't see a soul on the way there. Although it was lit up like midday, the gym was also empty. I mean, who works out at 3:00 a.m.?

Oh yeah, zombies.

After another quick steak snack, I dropped my bag by the treadmills. Then I stumbled to a corner with mats and mirrors. I started doing my regular gentle yoga moves. I felt my muscles stretching and relaxing.

"*AAAAAAAAAHHHHHHHHH!!!*" I sighed.

It felt so good to loosen up again!

Around 4:30 I headed back, feeling great. The halls were as silent as before. The door to our dorm was shut but not locked.

EEERRRRK

Everything was just as I left it.
Everyone was sound asleep.

CHAPTER 8

Sleep wouldn't have been an option even if I *were* still alive! Not after hearing Bella's creepy voice. I pretended I didn't hear her. (My headphones were on, so it was possible.) Then I slid on my eye mask and let my mind spin.

What did she mean, she was "on to me"? For all Bella knew, I could've just come back from the bathroom. But I could tell from her tone that she suspected more than that. What if she hadn't been asleep when I snuck out? What if she knew I'd been gone for hours? Could she possibly know *why*?

I snuggled farther under my blankets. Angela had guessed my undead secret, hadn't she? So had my little brother.

Bella was annoying, but she was smart. (Or at least, she usually was.) She might have the brains to figure it out. What would happen if the truth got into the hands of my enemy?

Visions of angry mobs danced in my head. I tried to ignore them by listening to my favorite musical soundtracks.

The moment the sun was up, I staggered out of bed and got my BOB. I needed extra time to fix my face before everyone else got to the bathrooms. Plus, I couldn't stand being in the room for another second!

I locked myself in a stall and did some quick face repairs to look alive. When I stepped out, I almost ran right into Bella.

"*EEEEEEEEP!*" I yelled.

"Wow, someone's on edge. Sleep well?" Bella asked. Her lip curled up on one side.

"Yeah," I replied slowly. "You?"

"Like the dead," she said. She looked at the red bag on my shoulder and sniffed. "You don't go anywhere without that thing, do you? It's like your security blanket."

More like my survival blanket, I thought. Out loud I said, "I just like to be prepared."

"Maybe. But if I didn't know better, I'd say you're hiding something," Bella said.

"Ha, ha," I said, trying to play it cool. I pushed past Bella and left the bathroom before she could ask more questions.

"Just don't cost us the game . . . Tulah," Bella said as the door closed. *Creepy!*

When I got back to our room, Nikki and Lacey were both up. They were whispering about Bella.

"Does she seem even worse today?" Lacey asked.

"Totally," Nikki said. "She fell right out of bed this morning. When I asked if she was all right, she practically growled at me!"

"Well, you know Bella," I said. "She'd probably die if anyone tried to help her do anything." I laughed nervously. Then I glanced at the door and dropped my voice. "Did Bella say anything to you guys? About last night?"

Nikki and Lacey shook their heads. "No. Why?" Lacey asked.

"Oh, nothing," I said. Inside I let out a sigh of relief. "Just thought I heard something."

Bella hadn't said anything about me sneaking out. If she told Ms. del Toro, I could be off the team for good. Then my parents would put me back in cross-country! But why wasn't Bella telling anyone?

"Are *you* OK, Tulah? You look like you saw a ghost." Lacey stared at me. "You're not catching whatever Bella has, are you?"

"No! I'm fine!" I said, trying to sound convincing. *I'm fine if having my future rest in Bella Gulosi's hands is fine.* (Hint: It's not!)

"Tulah? Hello?" Nikki stuck her face about an inch in front of mine. "Where are you, T?" she asked.

"Sorry." I shook my head to clear it. Our team and a few others were making flash cards to use for studying. Almost everyone already had a complete stack.

"We really need you to help pull the dead weight around here," Nikki whispered, tilting her head toward Bella.

Our captain was sitting at the end of the table. She was staring into space and hadn't completed a single card.

I looked down at my stack. It wasn't very thick either. I couldn't focus. All morning I'd been on edge, waiting for Bella to tell Ms. del Toro how I'd broken the rules. Bella wanted me off the team . . . didn't she?

"Listen up, A Team," Ms. del Toro said. She came to our table and crouched down. "I think we need a team meeting."

We all leaned in close. I got a whiff of something nasty.

Lacey wrinkled her nose. She smelled it too. She glared at the boys. "Don't you guys ever shower?"

"That is *not* me!" Josh shot back, crossing his arms. But I saw him sneak a sniff of his armpit.

"Gross," Bella said. She scooted her chair back from the group.

"Focus, team," Ms. del Toro said. "Bella and I had a chance to talk this morning. We both agreed that we need to make some changes."

I gulped. *When did they talk?* I thought. *How did I miss it?*

It didn't matter, though. I was about to be kicked out . . . in front of the entire A Team!

I closed my eyes and prepared to meet my doom.

"Bella admits that she hasn't been herself lately," Ms. del Toro continued. "There's a lot of pressure to deal with when you're captain. So, for the good of the team, she has agreed to step down."

I opened my eyes. That wasn't what I was expecting. It had caught the rest of the team by surprise too.

"But we need a captain!" Braden said. The he quickly held up his hands. "Not that I'm volunteering."

"Of course. I know many of you don't want to lead the group. So I suggested that Tulah should take over," Ms. del Toro said. "She's already proven to be a great help. What do you think, team?"

My jaw fell open. That was *definitely* not what I was expecting.

"Yeah, you'd be awesome, Tulah!" Lacey said. The other kids were nodding.

"B-but I just started," I stammered. "And the tournament is tomorrow. . . ." *And aren't you going to send me home?*

I was baffled. I looked at Bella, who looked at the floor. Then I looked at Nikki.

"You got this, Tulah!" Nikki said. She put her arm around my shoulder. "You're so good under pressure, and we know you've got the brains!"

I looked at Bella again. She had her mouth clamped shut. "You're really OK with this?" I asked.

Bella didn't meet my eyes, but she gave a quick, angry nod.

I couldn't believe it. She'd agreed to have *me* as captain? And I thought she was about to rat me out.

I didn't know what to say, so I just said, "Thanks."

"Don't thank me." Bella's pinched expression made it look like she could smell the same spoiled milk smell I could. "Just make sure we win."

CHAPTER 9

Bella didn't sit with the team at lunch, and I can't say I was surprised. Now I understood why she hadn't told Ms. del Toro about me sneaking out. It was like she'd said. The A Team needed me to win. But that didn't mean Bella had to like it.

To tell the truth, being captain wasn't as easy as I thought it'd be. During our afternoon practice sessions and speed rounds, I got the chance to try out my leadership skills. It was a tricky balance between telling people what to do and letting them do their own thing.

"Just say it," I whispered to Vincent when I could see he had the answer.

"Wait!" I had to tell Lacey almost every time. She'd blurt out the first thing that came to her mind. She usually got to the right answer eventually, but that first blurt could cost us in a real match.

Of course, the worst person to try to coach was Bella. She was totally useless. She just kept repeating the questions, and when she answered incorrectly, she got mad.

So as much as I dreaded bedtime, it was a relief to slide on my eye mask, slip on my headphones, and tuck into my bunk. Today had been exhausting.

Just one more night! I told myself.

After three hours, I turned off my podcast and listened to make sure everyone was asleep. Then I slowly started to stir, pausing with each rustle.

I made it out of the room without a hitch. As I lurched down the hall, my thoughts kept drifting back to Bella. I had figured out why she hadn't tattled on me. But I still couldn't get my head around why she was struggling so much on A Team.

During our practices, I could see that she wanted to win. She wanted to know the answers, but it was almost as if she couldn't get her brain to work. It was strange, and it definitely wasn't like her.

It almost made me feel sorry for Bella.

I pushed open the swinging door to the gym, dropped my BOB, and began to stretch. TBH, lately my life had been really complicated by my death. Maybe Bella had been acting differently for a while. But I just hadn't noticed because *I* had been acting so differently.

I dipped down into a forward bend and planted my hands on the yoga mat. I suddenly felt a cold breeze. The door had opened.

I looked up and gasped.

It was like the moment when you find that key puzzle piece. Everything clicked together in my mind.

Bella looked at me blankly. She tried to take a step forward and landed flat on her face.

"Oh!" I rushed over and unwedged her foot from the door. "You have to be careful! Any damage you do to yourself is permanent. What are you even doing here anyway?"

"*Hmph*," Bella snorted. "I'm following you because I need whatever is in your bag that's giving you all the answers."

I got a nose full of something nasty, and this time I recognized the smell. The stench was coming off Bella, and it smelled like rotting meat. It was the same stink that had been coming off *me* before Angela created her magical embalming smoothies.

"And what do you mean, I'm dead? You're not just cheating, you're crazy." Bella reached for my bag, but I yanked it away.

"*Cheating?*" I repeated. "Listen up, Bella. I am not cheating. I'm good at A Team because I'm smart. But you *are* dead.

Don't you know? Dead. Done-zo. Deceased. Departed."

Bella stopped reaching for my BOB. She just stood there blinking at me.

"So you don't have copies of all the retreat questions in your bag?" she asked.

I shook my head and opened the pack up so she could see for herself.

She dug through the bag, looking pretty confused. "OK, so maybe you aren't cheating. But you're still crazy. After all, if I'm so dead, how come I'm walking around? *Hmm?*" she asked snottily. "What do you even know about dead people?"

"A lot," I admitted. "Because I'm dead too. We're *walking* dead, and we died of the same thing. Remember that gross cafeteria veggie meal we got several weeks back?"

"They're all gross. How am I supposed to remember one over another?" Bella snipped.

"Remember the one that made you sick?" I said. "*Really* sick?"

Her face flickered with recognition.
"*Ew*. That one . . . What about it?"

"I think it killed us. Then we were reanimated," I said matter-of-factly.

Bella was still looking at me like I was blowing rainbow-colored balloons out of my nose. She needed more convincing.

"Here, pop quiz," I said. "Ever since you got sick, have you been able to eat?"

"Well, no. I haven't had much of an appetite since that sickness. What's that got to do with anything?" Bella huffed.

"OK, and how's your coordination?" I asked. "Have you been kind of stiff and clumsy?"

Bella crossed her arms. "How am I supposed to be graceful on zero sleep?"

"That answers my next question," I said. "You're not sleeping. So, here's my last. Is that smell coming from you?"

Bella got even paler. She looked furious. Then mortified. Then she collapsed into a heap on the yoga mats.

"I'm so embarrassed!" Bella moaned. "I was hoping nobody would notice. I shower all the time and brush my teeth nonstop, and I've been trying to keep my distance. The smell, everything—I didn't know what was happening. I couldn't find my symptoms online. I knew something wasn't right, and I wanted to figure it out. But I had no idea I was really a . . . a . . ."

"Zombie," I finished. "We're zombies."

Bella clenched her hands into fists. She gritted her teeth. "That's IMPOSSIBLE!" she shouted.

She slammed her fist down onto the treadmill next to her.

Her hand popped off her wrist and flew across the room.

Bella stared over at the runaway body part. Then she looked down at the bone sticking out of her wrist.

"Yeah," I said. "Sometimes pieces fall off. It's just one super fun side effect of being reanimated."

For once in her life, Bella was speechless.

I looked at my nemesis, and then at the precious BOB Angela had put together for me. My friends had helped me so much in figuring out all this weird undead business.

But Bella had no one, and she was seriously struggling. We weren't even close to being friends, but I knew how terrifying being a zombie was, even *with* help.

I couldn't leave her on her own.

So with a sigh, I ruffled around in my bag. I pulled out a piece of freeze-dried beef from my small stash.

"Here." I handed it to Bella.

She suddenly forgot all about her hand and went after the meat like a rabid dog. I gave her another piece, and she started to pull herself together.

"Why is this so good?" Bella asked between bites.

"It's raw meat that's been dried out. Raw meat is pretty much all we can eat," I explained as I went to grab her hand. "You need meat to keep your grumpy moods in check and your mind working—"

"So that's why I've been feeling so dumb!" Bella said. "I've had stupid zombie brains!" She got quiet again. "We don't *eat* brains, do we?" She stared at me. "Is that why you joined A Team? Because you wanted smart, healthy brains?"

"NO!" I shouted. "Never. We are *not* brain-eating zombies, and we are definitely not *people*-eating zombies."

"That's good," Bella said. "Because I want to be well-fed and never feel stupid again."

"Well, just eat normal animal meat, and you'll be good," I said. "You may also want to polish up your sewing skills. They come in *handy.*"

Bella didn't laugh at my pun. So I just pulled out my emergency sewing kit and got to work putting her hand back on.

"It doesn't hurt at all," Bella whispered as I pulled the needle through her skin.

"Yeah, that's one perk, at least," I said. After I tied off the last stitch, I dug out my precious smoothie thermos from the bag. I gave it to her. "This little mix stops your corpse from breaking down more. It'll help keep you in one piece, and it'll help with the stench."

Bella sniffed. "Is it pickle juice?"

"Formaldehyde," I told her. "Plus other embalming liquid. I get it from Angela. Now, if you're not dead, it could kill you. . . ."

Bella tipped the thermos back and took several big gulps. She wiped her mouth with her newly reattached hand. "So how long have you known you were . . . ?" she asked.

"I pretty much figured out I was dead the first week," I said. "With a little help. I didn't know about you until right now."

"So you've had a bunch of time to figure this out. And, like, a whole team helping you?" Bella asked. "Angela and who else?"

I could hear an edge in Bella's voice. She was used to being jealous, but she wasn't used to accepting help.

"Not that *I* need help," Bella continued. "Now that I know the basics, I can figure it all out on my own." She thrust the thermos back at me and almost spilled what little was left.

I rolled my eyes. Apparently there were some things even death couldn't change. "Fine," I said. "Have it your way. But you need to be careful. You can't tell anyone the truth about me, and you probably shouldn't tell anyone about you either. It would put us both in real danger!"

"Oh, but you can tell the whole world?" she asked.

"Angela figured out my secret before I did. Her family deals with death. But if more people know about us, we are not going to have a happily ever afterlife," I said.

I decided right then not to tell Bella that Nikki and Jaybee were also in on my secret. Our secret.

"People hate the undead," I added. "They think we're the sign of a zombie apocalypse. Haven't you seen the movies?"

The look of devastation on Bella's face as it all started to sink in made me turn away. I remembered that moment, when I realized the world would never see me in the same way.

I pulled one more thing out of my pack and handed it to Bella. It was my dog-eared copy of *Zombie Boy Z*. Jaybee had given me his favorite comic so that I could learn all about being undead. Now it was time to pass it on to a new zombie trainee.

"You have some studying to do," I said, tossing the comic into her lap. "I mean, if you want to win at this zombie game."

Bella smiled, just a tiny bit. It was the first smile I'd seen on her face in a long time.

"Now you're starting to sound like a captain," she said. "But . . . why do you want to help me?"

"Because I still have a heart, even if it's not beating. I know what you're going through, and, oh yeah . . ." I held out my arms in front of me, and swayed back and forth. ". . . the A Team needs your brrraaaiiinnns!"

CHAPTER 10

"Where have you two been?" Nikki asked when Bella and I came back to the room in our PJs. It was 7 a.m., and everyone was starting to get up.

"We've been trading study tips," I said casually.

When the other girls weren't looking, I gave Nikki a wink. She shot me back a questioning look and mouthed the word *what?*

I was dying to tell her that Bella was a zombie and that I'd spent the morning giving her a crash course in the undead. For the first time in her life (er, death), Bella had actually listened to me. She hadn't liked it, but she had listened.

"I thought maybe Bella could use some coaching," I said. I saw Bella's shoulders stiffen. (The last thing she wanted to admit was that she needed help doing *anything*.) So I quickly added a compliment. "And she gave me some captain pointers too."

"Awesome, you guys! Just in time for the tournament," Lacey said. "We're going to need all the brains we've got to win today. Are you two ready for breakfast?"

"Oh, uh, we already ate. I brought some energy bars," I explained. "You guys go ahead. We'll meet you later."

There was one last thing I wanted to share with Bella. When the girls were gone, I took out my corpse makeup. The foundation color was all wrong for Bella, but I had a few things that could help her. I used a little blush to put color back in her cheeks and a highlighting pencil to cover the dark circles under her eyes.

I spun her around to face the mirror in the dorm, and the two of us gazed into it.

The makeup job wasn't perfect, but the former captain looked a lot less dead. Bella lifted her chin.

"I'm back!" she announced. "And I'm ready to kill it!"

The tournament started after breakfast. For the first time since I'd joined A Team, everyone was ready to compete!

I tried to find a minute alone to tell Nikki what had happened in the "study session" Bella and I'd had, but we were never alone. Although the look on Nikki's face when Bella buzzed in and got the very first question right was priceless. It was almost worth keeping the secret for.

"Bella's back?" she whispered to me.

"From the dead," I told her.

Nikki blinked. "You mean . . . ?"

I nodded. "The horrible Mystery Meal struck again. All she needed was a little zombie food."

The rest of the team was just as surprised as Nikki to see Bella back on her game.

We blew through the first two rounds of the tournament like they were nothing. We easily won both. I think the other teams were caught completely off guard. But in the next round, the final, they'd be expecting our A game.

"Great job, everybody!" I said.

Our whole team was gathered outside the auditorium. We were about to go onstage and face off against Amityville for the championship. Vincent was moving from one foot to the other. Nikki was nibbling her lip. The pressure was getting to them.

"Just remember, we are all in this together! Don't buzz in until you're sure. We don't want to hand Amityville any chances for easy points." I tried to sound encouraging and captainlike. "If we put our best foot forward, there is no team that can beat us."

Josh and Vincent nodded.

"Yeah," Lacey agreed. "We got this."

Bella just rolled her eyes and crossed her arms.

We broke the circle and walked inside. All the other retreat kids were seated in the auditorium seats. Onstage were two tables, one for each team.

Four of the A Teamers took the seats at the table. The rest of us took seats next to the curtain. Only four kids could compete at a time. So Braden, Lacey, Chris, and Josh were playing the first half.

We got this! I repeated to myself as the moderator started reading.

Ten questions later, I wasn't so sure. Amityville was matching us question for question. The score was tied.

Now, at the half, we were switching things up. Braden, Lacey, Chris, and Josh had done all they could. It was up to Nikki, Bella, Vincent, and me to bring in the win.

We traded seats, and I looked down the table. TBH, my team seemed kind of stressed. Nikki was starting to nibble again, and Vincent looked like he wanted to cry. I turned to Bella. I knew I could count on her under pressure. Right?

The beginning signal sounded, and I tried to focus on the moderator's question.

"Mason Dixon!" Nikki buzzed in, and we high-fived.

"Fifty-two!" Vincent got out a good answer on the next one.

"Ultraviolet!" A pink-haired girl on the Amityville side scored a point.

"The speed of light!" The Amityville team scored *again*.

If I could still sweat, I would have been sweating buckets. It was so close!

I looked at Bella and freaked out a little more. Her sour face was back.

She hates to lose, I thought. Then I thought of something else. *OMG, I think she's hungry!*

I'd been sneaking snacks all day. But I had totally forgotten to give Bella anything since breakfast. . . .

Now Bella's zombie brains were back!

I had one last dried beef snack in my pocket.

CRINKLE CRINKLE

"This is our last question," the moderator said. "For the game, the parents of this hero were Thetis and Peleus."

Nikki bit her bottom lip. Vincent drummed his fingers. Bella twitched. I had a guess, but we all knew mythology was Bella's specialty. I had to trust that the beef worked and that she'd get the answer.

"During the Trojan War, this hero was shot by Paris," the moderator continued.

The pink-haired girl suddenly buzzed in. "Theseus!" she shouted.

The moderator drew in a sharp breath. "I'm sorry, that's incorrect." She continued with the question. "His mother dipped him into the river Styx to make him invincible. Still this hero was left with one weakness."

Bella lurched for the buzzer. She hit it so hard I worried she would lose her hand again. "Achilles!" she shouted.

As soon as I heard the answer, I knew it was right. Bella had done it! She'd clinched the game.

"Yes!" the moderator said. "The victory goes to Evansville's A Team! Great game!"

The audience cheered. After a lot of hugging and jumping, the A Team filed backstage. Ms. del Toro was waiting for us.

"Fantastic job, everyone. And, Bella, you were wonderful! You're back to your old self!" she said, patting her ace student.

"No, Ms. del Toro, you're looking at the *new* me!" Bella held her arms up and did a clumsy twirl so everyone could admire her greatness. If you were looking for it, you might've noticed a slightly pickled scent.

"Nice work," I told her.

It felt strange to be complimenting my nemesis. But it had been a strange night, and a strange morning.

Maybe, just maybe, Bella and I weren't going to be enemies anymore. After all, we were the only two zombies in the world (as far as I knew). Maybe now the two of us could just be friends.

"Yes," Bella agreed. "I did do nice work."

I waited for her to thank me for sneaking her the meat snack, or to tell me I'd done well as captain, or that she was glad I'd joined the team. Or *something*.

Instead she gave me her signature sneer.

"I mean, our special little 'study session' was useful and all, but I got this." Bella shot me a look that let me know *exactly* what she meant. She didn't want my help on A Team, or on anything else. "So we won't be needing you to lead A Team anymore, Tulah. I'm taking back my role as captain."

My mouth fell open so fast, I thought my jaw might pop off.

Bella smiled, then turned and lurched toward the rest of the team. They were still celebrating and hadn't heard the news.

But suddenly I didn't care who was captain. I was just happy to be part of a team. Happy (kind of) Bella had her brains back. And happy to have survived the academic retreat, even as a dead girl.

TULAH'S TERMS

Bug Out Bag (or BOB)—just like Angela said, this is a pack with everything a person needs to survive for seventy-two hours. People have these so they're prepared for emergencies like fires, floods, and other natural disasters. My BOB is to survive sleepovers.

corpse—simply put, a dead body

dorm—a place were students live in college. Sharing one of these tiny rooms with Nikki would've been fun. But sharing one with Bella too? Not so much.

embalming—able to stop dead things from rotting. Formaldehyde is a kind of embalming liquid. If a living person drank anything that's embalming, it'd kill them. Good thing I'm already dead.

formaldehyde—a gas that when dissolved in water makes the perfect mixture to stop most anything dead from rotting

funeral home—the place where dead people are prepared for burial or cremation. It's also the perfect place for me to get patched up. (Thanks, Angela!)

lumber—to move very slowly and awkwardly. We're talking zero grace.

lurch—to move with a jerky motion, and how zombies walk. I'm not going to win a dance contest anytime soon.

moderator—in academic team competitions, this is the person who reads the questions, leads the round, and has all the answers

mortified—beyond embarrassed

nemesis—the number-one enemy of your life. My nemesis, Bella Gulosi, is simply the worst.

reanimate—to bring back to life. I'm still trying to figure out how it worked for me!

routine—a way of doing activities and tasks in a particular order. My nighttime zombie routine sets me up for success throughout the day!

sabotage—to cause another a person to fail, usually by doing mean and sneaky things. Bella is definitely not above playing dirty.

vegetarian—a person who doesn't eat meat. Hard to believe my raw-meat-loving self was ever satisfied with just vegetables, fruits, grains, nuts, eggs, and dairy.

zombie apocalypse—when a whole bunch of zombies rise up and attack all the living. It's worse than the middle school mean girls' rude attitudes at lunch, but just barely.

USE YOUR BRAAAAINS!

Don't worry, I won't eat them.

... and angrier.

Time!

1. Be a mind reader! Tell me, what is Bella thinking here? What in the art helps show her emotions? For an extra challenge, try writing thought bubbles for her.

2. Bella wants to do everything on her own. But I'm not sure that's a good idea. What do you think? Help me write a letter to Bella arguing why she should or shouldn't accept help. Be sure to use examples—that'll help convince her!

3. EEK! Hearing that voice really creeped me out. Why did it make me nervous? Who's talking? (Flip to pages 70-71 if you need a reminder.)

I'm on to you, Tulah. . . .

4. As my dad likes to say, teamwork makes the dream work! Talk about a time you and others worked together to accomplish a goal. What was good about being in a group? What was hard?

5. I can't believe I missed the fact that Bella was a member of the undead! TBH, it's kind of obvious now that I think about it. Were you surprised too, or did you know all along? Go back through the story and look for hints that Bella was actually a zombie.

6. I've discovered stories of all different kinds of zombies. Some are slow, but some are fast. Some are mindless, but some can talk (like me!). Create your own zombie. What abilities do they have? What do they look like? What causes people to become undead? I need details!

OMG, ZOMBIE!

After eating a suspicious school meal, I feel different. REALLY different. Find out how my undead life began!

REALLY ROTTEN DRAMA

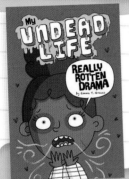

I'm dealing with a BFF crisis, my first-ever (stage) kiss, and my rotting zombie body! Can I put an end to this stinky situation?

TOTAL FREAK-OUT

No meat equals one grumpy zombie. Can I get enough food to keep my mood under control before the school dance?

GOT BRAINS?

I'm going on a retreat with the academic team (and my worst nemesis, Bella Gulosi!). Will I survive the weekend?

Find them all at
MYCAPSTONE.COM

About the Author

Emma T. Graves has authored more than ninety books for children and has written about characters both living and dead. When she's not writing, Emma enjoys watching classic horror movies, taking long walks in the nearby cemetery, and storing up food in her cellar. She is prepared for the zombie apocalypse.

About the Illustrator

Binny Boo, otherwise known as Ellie O'Shea, is a coffee addict, avid snowboarder, puppy fanatic— and an illustrator. Her love for art started at a young age. She spent her childhood drawing, watching cartoons, creating stories, and eating too many sweets for her own good. She graduated from Plymouth University in 2015 with a degree in illustration. She now lives in Worcester, UK, and feels so lucky that she gets to spend her days doing what she adores.